Lizzy Lightning Bug
Lizzy la luciérnaga

Learn to Read Series
Book 17

Cataloging-in-Publication Data

Sargent, Dave, 1941–
    Lizzy lightning bug = Lizzy la luciérnaga /
by Dave and Pat Sargent ; illustrated by
Laura Robinson.—Prairie Grove, AR :
Ozark Publishing, c2004.
    p. cm. (Learn to read series ; 17)

    Bilingual.
    Cover title.
    SUMMARY: A little lightning bug cannot
find her light. She cannot go to her friend's
party because she cannot see to fly at night.
    ISBN 1-56763-993-3 (hc)
           1-56763-994-1 (pbk)

    [1. Animals—Fiction.] I. Sargent, Pat,
1936– II. Robinson, Laura, 1973– ill. III. Title.
IV. Series.
    PZ7.S2465Ic 2004
    [E]—dc21   00-012635

Printed in the United States of America

Lizzy Lightning Bug
Lizzy la luciérnaga

Learn to Read Series
Book 17

By Dave and Pat Sargent

Illustrated by Laura Robinson

Ozark Publishing, Inc.
P.O. Box 228
Prairie Grove, AR 72753

Dave and Pat Sargent, authors of the extremely popular Animal Pride Series, plus many other Accelerated Reader books, visit schools all over the United States, free of charge.

If you would like to have Dave and Pat visit your school, please ask your librarian to call 1-800-321-5671.

Lizzy Lightning Bug
Lizzy la luciérnaga

Learn to Read Series
Book 17

I am a lightning bug. My name is Lizzy.

Yo soy una luciérnaga. Me llamo Lizzy.

I have a problem. I am in a real tizzy.

Yo tengo un problema. Yo estoy nervioso.

I should shine at night, but I cannot find my light.

Yo debo brillar en la noche, pero no puedo encontrar mi luz.

My mama has a light, and so does my dad.

Mi mamá tiene una luz, y mi papá también.

I am so sad. Sally's party is tonight.

Yo estoy muy triste. La fiesta de Sally es ésta noche.

I cannot go without my light.

No puedo ir sin mi luz.

I looked on my wings and on top of my head.

La busqué en mis alas y en mi coronilla.

I looked behind my legs and behind my tail.

La busqué detrás de mis patas y detrás de mi cola.

My brother laughs. He thinks it is funny.

Mi hermano se ríe. Piensa que es cómico.

If I fell in the water, I could lie there and rot.

Si me caería en el agua, yo yacería allí y me pudriría.

I could hit a tree and get caught on a limb.

Yo podría chocar con un árbol y estaría atrapada en una rama.

11

The chance of being found would be very slim.

La posibilidad de estar encontrada sería escasa.

I will sit here at my door and watch for kitty cats.

Me sentaré aquí en mi puerta y estaré al acecho de gatitos.

13

Do cats eat lightning bugs. Or do they eat rats?

¿Los gatos comen luciérnagas? ¿O comen ratas?

I worry about things like birds, bats, and cats.

Me preocupo de cosas como pájaros, murciélagos y gatos.

I will touch my tummy and say the magic word.

Yo tocaré mi barriga y diré la fórmula mágica.

"Let my light shine, please!" Look! It worked!

<<Favor de dejar mi luz brillar.>> ¡Mira! ¡Salió bien!

My light is shining. I can see!

Mi luz brilla. ¡Yo puedo ver!